For Suzie and Ollie, love from your big monster - James

For the 3 little monsters, Georgia, Martha & Bella.
Always wash your smelly socks! - M.C.

Published by Top That! Publishing plc
Tide Mill Way, Woodbridge, Suffolk, IP12 1AP, UK
www.topthatpublishing.com
Concept & Text copyright © James McKnight 2011
Illustration copyright © Mark Chambers 2011
All rights reserved
0 2 4 6 8 9 7 5 3 1
Printed and bound in China

Creative Director – Simon Couchman
Editorial Director – Daniel Graham

Written by James McKnight
Illustrated by Mark Chambers

ISBN 978-1-84956-450-2

A catalogue record for this book is available from the British Library
Printed and bound in China

McDOOGLE'S MONSTER FARM
The Day the Gogglynipper Escaped

Written by James McKnight

Illustrated by Mark Chambers

McDoogle's Monster Farm Field Guide:

Out in the countryside, far away from any towns or cities is a very unusual farm. This farm is different to any other farm. On this farm you won't find cows or sheep or chickens. On this farm they don't grow potatoes or carrots. It is the most unusual farm of all ... it is McDoogle's Monster Farm!

Farmer McDoogle keeps monsters of all shapes and sizes on his monster farm.

Gogglynippers are the biggest monsters on the farm. They eat very smelly socks. They are very dramatic monsters, and always overreact to any event. They can get very angry, but can also be the happiest monsters on the farm.

Funderbigglers are big, scary birds covered with multi-coloured feathers. They can't fly as their wings are far too small, and their bodies are very big. This doesn't stop them from trying to fly though; they are always climbing up on top of walls and fences and jumping off, sometimes with disastrous results.

Nooglebooglers are medium-sized monsters with bright neon fur. They eat the leaves from the difflebug plant which Farmer McDoogle grows on the farm. Nooglebooglers glow in the dark, but only when they eat enough difflebug leaves.

Difflebug leaves are from the difflebug plant. The difflebug plant is very dangerous. Difflebug plants have big flowers with teeth that can bite. Picking the leaves from the difflebug plant is very difficult. Farmer McDoogle grows a field full of them to feed the Nooglebooglers he rears on the farm.

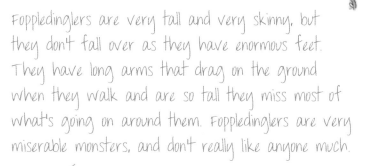

Foppledinglers are very tall and very skinny, but they don't fall over as they have enormous feet. They have long arms that drag on the ground when they walk and are so tall they miss most of what's going on around them. Foppledinglers are very miserable monsters, and don't really like anyone much.

Diggle helps Farmer McDoogle out on his farm. He's an expert at caring for the Gogglynippers, the biggest and scariest of all the monsters on McDoogle's Monster Farm.

One day, Diggle was out on the hillside blowing his special whistle, rounding up the Gogglynippers.

Wheeeeeeeeeeeeeeeeeeeeeee!

Diggle counted the Gogglynippers, 'One, two, three, four, five, six, seven, eight, nine ...
Only nine Gogglynippers! Oh no!' said Diggle.
'We're missing a Gogglynipper!'

How was Diggle going to tell Farmer McDoogle that he had lost a Gogglynipper, the biggest, scariest monster on the farm?

Diggle decided that he had to find the missing Gogglynipper before it got dark. He headed up into the hills with his trusty dog, Noober.

Diggle searched up and down the hills, blowing on his special whistle as hard as he could. As it got darker, Noober began to get scared, and howled along with Diggle's whistle.

hoooowwwi

Suddenly, Diggle slipped on a big pile of mud and fell onto his bottom with a squelch. 'Hang on a minute,' thought Diggle. 'This pile of mud smells very bad.' Diggle knew of only one thing that could smell that bad …

… Gogglynipper poo! A big, steaming pile of Gogglynipper poo! A clue!

Then Diggle spotted some enormous footprints, made by an enormous foot with three enormous toes.

Diggle followed the footprints into a big cave. He edged slowly and carefully into the cave as he knew that Gogglynippers are not only the biggest monsters, they are also the most dramatic.

Suddenly, there was a big, loud roar and the
Gogglynipper came running out of the cave.

He ran right up to Diggle, opened his mouth wide and licked him from top to bottom! (What Diggle didn't know is that even the biggest monsters can be scared of the dark, so the Gogglynipper was very happy to see him.)

Diggle attached a lead
to the Gogglynipper
and began the journey
back to the farm to
put the monster to bed.

Diggle could hear all of the other monsters snoring very loudly, even though he was very far away over the hills. (Monsters snore very loudly.)

When they were halfway home, the Gogglynipper started to act strangely. He sniffed the air and got very excited. Then he started jumping up and down, and began to pull on his lead. Diggle suddenly noticed a smell in the air. It was the smell of very smelly old socks. (Gogglynippers love eating very smelly old socks!)

Yum!

Yum!

Woof! Woof!

The Gogglynipper sped off in the direction that the smell was coming from. 'Noooooooooo!' screamed Diggle, as he was pulled along, hanging onto the end of the lead. Noober chased after them barking!

Help!

They raced faster and faster!
Diggle couldn't even see what
direction they were going.

Soon they arrived back
at the farm. The Gogglynipper
raced straight past the monster enclosure,
round the corner to the farmhouse, and
straight up to the farmhouse window.

Hanging out of the window were two very large, very smelly, old socks!

Just as the Gogglynipper was about to bite the two very large feet, they disappeared and Farmer McDoogle stuck his head out of the window! 'What do you think you're doing with that Gogglynipper?' he said.

Once Diggle explained what had happened, Farmer McDoogle laughed and said, 'It's a good job I only wash my socks once a week!'

Farmer McDoogle helped Diggle put the Gogglynipper into the enclosure with the other monsters, and they all went to bed. After washing their socks, of course.

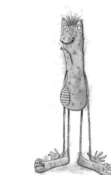

If you enjoyed this book, then you'll love

'Only Nooglebooglers Glow in the Dark'!

Illustrated by award-winning artist, Mark Chambers.

ISBN 978-1-84956-451-9

When there is a power cut on the farm, only the Nooglebooglers can shine a light on the matter.

ISBN 978-1-84956-303-1

Snuffletrump the piglet will try anything to get rid of his hiccups!

ISBN 978-1-84956-305-5

The animals are making a hullabaloo in this humorous picture storybook!

ISBN 978-1-84956-245-4

Unique illustrations capture the loving bond between two best friends!

ISBN 978-1-84956-304-8

Milly the meerkat learns a very important lesson in this classic tale.

ISBN 978-1-84956-302-4

Follow the antics of the escaped zoo animals as they cause pandamonium!

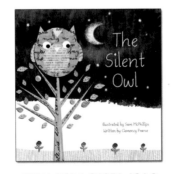

ISBN 978-1-84956-424-3

A wise owl refuses to bow to peer pressure in this amusing, rhyming tale.

ISBN 978-1-84956-438-0

A fantastical tale about unruly, morning hair and a mischievous fairy.

ISBN 978-1-84956-100-6

Comic wordplay explores what a toucan or toucan't do.

Available from all good bookstores or visit www.topthatpublishing.com
Look for Top That! Apps in the Apple iTunes Store